PAUL MASON

SKATE MONKEY

DEMON ATTACK

ILLUSTRATED BY
ROBIN BOYDEN

BLOOMSBURY EDUCATION
AN IMPRINT OF BLOOMSBURY

LONDON OXFORD NEW YORK NEW DELHI SYDNEY

SKATE MONKEY

Monkey and his friends, Zu and Sandy, lived in the Jade Emperor's Cloud Palace. But they played all sorts of tricks on people, so, as a punishment, the Jade Emperor sent them down to Earth.

They can only return to the Cloud Palace if they prove that they can use their magical powers for good...

CONTENTS

Story inspired by *Monkey* by
Wu Ch' Êng-Ên, c1500–1582

Chapter One

Sam Clarke ran down the empty school hallway. It was Monday morning. He was late.

Sam saw a dark figure at the end of the hall.

It was the headteacher. She stood with her arms folded.

Sam smiled. Luckily for him, the headteacher was his Aunt Jill. "Sorry I'm late, Aunt Jill. Mum's car wouldn't start," said Sam. He held out the note from his mum.

The headteacher didn't smile back. "Lunchtime detention," she said crossly.

"But Aunt Jill," said Sam, "I have a note."

"I don't care about your note," said the headteacher. "Now get to your classroom."

"Aunt Jill?" said Sam.

"Call me Miss Clarke!" said the headteacher. She stared at Sam with cold eyes. It was as if she didn't even know him.

"Yes, Miss Clarke," said Sam. He crept off to his classroom.

Chapter Two

A few days later, Sam went to the park. He found his friends, Monkey, Sandy and Zu. They were practising tricks on their skateboards. Sam needed their help.

"What do you mean, your aunt is acting strange?" said Monkey.

"She used to be really kind and fair," said Sam. "But now Aunt Jill has turned into the meanest headteacher ever. All the students are scared. Even the teachers are frightened of her."

"So what? Maybe she is just in a bad mood," said Sandy.

"It's more than that." Sam shook his head. "I know this is going to sound weird, but I don't think that the headteacher is my Aunt Jill at all."

"What do you mean?" asked Zu.

"The headteacher looks like my aunt. She sounds like my aunt. But it isn't her. I can tell," said Sam. "And I haven't told you the strangest thing of all."

"What's that?" asked Sandy.

"It's her reflection in the mirror," said Sam.

"What about it?" asked Zu.

"She doesn't have one. If she stands in front of a mirror, her reflection is invisible," said Sam.

"You are joking!" said Monkey.

"I saw her walk past the mirror in the hall," said Sam. "There was no reflection. I almost screamed. But no one else noticed. I thought I must have been seeing things."

"Wow!" said Zu. "Sounds like you really need our help."

"And the Jade Emperor did say if we did good things he would let us go back home," said Monkey.

"How about we come to your school?" said Sandy.

"Back to school?" said Zu. "Do we have to?"

Chapter Three

The next day, Monkey, Sandy and Zu met Sam outside the school. Monkey looked uncomfortable in his uniform. His tail kept poking out from under his trousers.

"This way," said Sam. They went up the stairs.

There was a poster outside Sam's classroom. Monkey stopped to read it.

Brook Street School

100 Year Anniversary Celebration

Today! 5pm

VIP Guest: Prime Minister Ellen Jones

"This school is 100 years old. The Prime Minister is coming to our special celebration tonight. Everyone is really excited," said Sam.

Suddenly, a dark shadow appeared in front of them. It was the headteacher, Miss Clarke. She looked very cross. She pointed at Monkey.

"Me? What did I do?" asked Monkey, quickly hiding his tail.

"Your uniform is a mess," said the headteacher. "Lunchtime detention!"

The headteacher stared at them. Then she marched off down the hall to shout at some other students.

"See what I mean?" said Sam.

"Well, at least this gives me a chance to take a closer look at her," said Monkey.

Chapter Four

The detention room was full of students. They sat at their desks, writing out lines: "I must do as I am told," copied out a hundred times each. Monkey quickly found a seat at the back.

"You are late!" said the headteacher crossly. "Two hundred lines for you!"

"Ouch," said Monkey. He started writing. When the headteacher wasn't looking, he took out his fiery-eyes glasses. The glasses let him see through any disguise. Monkey put the glasses on.

Monkey only just stopped himself from yelling out.

At the front of the classroom stood a skeleton
with long, white, bones. The skeleton wore white

robes. She carried a sharp sword. Her eyes glowed like fire.

This wasn't Sam's aunt. This was a demon. An evil white-bone demon – the worst kind.

Monkey took a deep breath. He tried to stay calm. "So what has happened to Sam's aunt?" he thought.

Chapter Five

Later, Monkey met his friends in the lunch room. They sat down to eat their lunch.

"I have terrible news," said Monkey.

"Sam is right. The headteacher isn't his aunt. She's not even human. She's a white-bone demon."

Sam almost spat out his food. "A demon!"

"White-bone demons are shape-shifters," said Sandy. "They can take any shape they want."

"So that is why she doesn't have a reflection," said Zu.

"But what about Aunt Jill," said Sam. "What has happened to her?"

"I bet the demon is keeping her prisoner somewhere," said Sandy.

"So what do we do?" asked Sam.

"We flatten the demon, that's what we do," said Monkey. He reached into his jacket. He pulled out a pen. "Full charge," he said. The pen flashed and crackled as it changed shape.

The pen grew and grew. Soon it was the size of a baseball bat. Monkey spun it around in his hand. Some of the other students stopped eating their lunch and stared at Monkey.

"Put that away!" whispered Sandy. "If we fight the demon now, we might never find Sam's aunt."

"Good point," said Monkey. He said some more magic words and the bat turned back into a pen.

"We could call the police," said Sam.

"They wouldn't believe us," said Sandy.

"Sandy is right. It's up to us to fix this. But why is the demon disguising herself as a headteacher?" asked Monkey.

Chapter Six

After lunch, Monkey, Sandy and Zu found an empty classroom.

"We need disguises. Then we can spy on the demon and find Sam's aunt," said Monkey. "I will use a shape-shifting spell!"

Monkey said the magic words. There was a sudden bright light. Monkey disappeared. He turned into a fly.

"A fly? Yuck," said Sandy.

"This way we can go wherever we want," buzzed Monkey.

"I guess you're right," said Sandy. She cast a spell and she turned into a fly.

Another spell, another flash, and Zu became a fly too.

"Let's go," buzzed Monkey. The three friends flew down the hall. They landed on the wall outside the office. The bell rang for the end of lunch. Students made their way along the hall. No one saw the flies on the wall. At last, the headteacher came out of her office.

"Straight to your classrooms!" she shouted at the students. Then she marched off down the hallway.

"Come on!" buzzed Monkey. He flew off after her.

The three friends spied on the headteacher for the rest of the afternoon. They followed her from classroom to classroom. They spied on her as she yelled at students and teachers.

They spied on her in the hall
as she led the practice for the
Prime Minister's visit.

"But where is she keeping Sam's aunt?" asked Sandy.

Then, right at the end of the day, they saw the headteacher go into a storeroom and shut the door behind her. They waited.

"She has been in there a long time," buzzed Zu.

At last the headteacher came out. She locked the storeroom door behind her.

"I bet that's where Sam's aunt is," said Monkey.

Chapter Seven

Monkey and the others changed back into their normal shapes, and waited for Sam after school. They made sure the headteacher wasn't around. They went to the storeroom.

The door was locked. Monkey whispered another magic spell – the lock-opening spell. The lock clicked open.

"Come on," said Monkey.

Inside the storeroom it was dark. There were some stairs at the back. The friends went down the stairs into a basement. They could see a shape in the corner.

"Aunt Jill!" cried Sam. He ran over and gave his aunt a hug. She was tied up with ropes. Sam untied her. "I've brought friends," he said.

"What happened to you?" asked Monkey.

Aunt Jill shivered. "That demon kidnapped me one morning before school. She grabbed hold of me and dragged me down here. Then she changed into my shape. The demon has been keeping me prisoner ever since."

"What does she want?" asked Sandy.

"I don't know," said Aunt Jill. "But the demon said it would be all over the news tonight."

"What does that mean?" asked Zu.

"I know,' said Sandy. "It's the anniversary celebration tonight and the Prime Minister is coming."

"Of course!' said Monkey. "The demon wants to get to Prime Minister Jones! What time does she come?"

"Five o'clock," said Sam.

Monkey looked at his watch. He saw it was four thirty. "Let's go!"

Chapter Eight

The friends ran up the stairs. They ran out of the store room. A crowd of students and parents were waiting outside the hall for the celebration to start. Everyone wanted to meet Prime Minister Jones.

"You two go outside to meet the Prime Minister," said Monkey to Sam and his aunt. "We will go and stop the demon before she can carry out her evil plan."

Monkey, Sandy and Zu ran to the hall. Monkey opened the lock and quickly shut the door behind them.

The demon was on the stage. She was making sure her trap was ready. "What are you doing in here?" she said crossly. "You have already been in trouble once today. I will ring your parents!"

Monkey laughed. "I don't think so. We know who you are, white-bone demon."

Monkey pulled out his pen. "Full charge," he said. Soon the pen was the size of a baseball bat. Monkey spun it around in his hand.

Sandy got out her smartphone. "Upgrade," she cried. The smartphone changed shape.

It became a huge metal pole. Sandy twirled the pole above her head like a helicopter.

Zu reached into his jacket. He pulled out a fork. "Supersize!" he called. The fork glowed and turned into a huge rake.

The demon laughed and changed into her true shape. Now, instead of a headteacher, there stood a giant skeleton. Her bones shook. Her eyes glowed. The demon threw her sword from hand to hand. "I am going to kidnap the Prime Minister, and take her shape. Then I will rule the country!" she shouted. "You can't stop me!"

"Time to crunch some bones," said Monkey.

Chapter Nine

Monkey leapt at the skeleton. He brought his bat down hard. The demon blocked him with her sword. She spun round and knocked Monkey off the stage.

Sandy swung her pole. It went right through the skeleton. But nothing happened. The demon laughed and pushed Sandy over.

Then Zu attacked with his rake. The demon danced around, dodging him. Then she kicked Zu to the ground.

"Harder than you thought?" laughed the demon. Her bones shook.

"It's not over yet!" spat Monkey. "Now!" he shouted. Monkey and Sandy charged together. Before they could reach her, the demon jumped into the air. Monkey and Sandy crashed into each other. They fell into a heap.

"Ha ha!" laughed the demon. She hung from the lights above the stage.

"Why don't you watch where you're going?" Monkey said to Sandy.

"Why don't you?" said Sandy.

"Don't worry, I'll take care of her," said Zu. He jumped up at the demon on the lights. The demon smacked him right back down. Zu fell into a heap on the floor.

"That must have hurt," laughed the demon. She jumped down onto the stage. "Now, time to finish the fight."

Monkey said, "I've had enough of this. Let's get some help." He quickly pulled three hairs out of his head. He blew on the hairs. He said the words of a magic spell. There was a burst of light.

Then there were three more Monkeys on the stage. Each Monkey held a bat.

The Monkeys closed in on the demon. "You are in a whole lot of trouble," they said.

"Get her!" yelled Monkey. Sandy and the Monkeys attacked together. They charged into the demon. Wham! The demon screamed. They swung their bats. Bam! The demon fell down. Crash! Sandy struck the demon with her pole. The demon flew through the air and into a row of chairs. She lay in a heap.

"I think this show is over," said Sandy.

"Think again!" laughed the demon. She got to her feet. Then, before they could stop her, the demon jumped onto a high window ledge.

"See you next time," she laughed. The demon opened a window, climbed out, and was gone.

"I so hope there isn't a next time," said Zu, rubbing his head.

Monkey said some magic words. The other monkeys disappeared. He put the hairs back on his head. "Let's get this hall ready for the celebration," he said.

***

Monkey, Zu and Sandy were at the skate park learning new tricks.

Sam was back at school. The Prime
Minister's visit had been a huge success.
Everyone cheered after the Prime Minister's
speech. Aunt Jill was back in charge of the
school, and the demon was gone.

"So, do you think we have done enough good deeds to go home now?" asked Zu.

"We did save a school and a Prime Minister," said Sandy. "And we stopped a demon."

"Who knows? I guess we will just have to wait and see," Monkey laughed. "I'm just glad to be out of that school uniform."

Bonus Bits!

What is a Prime Minister?

- A prime minister is the head of a government in a country.
- The role was introduced and developed in the UK in the 1700s.
- The Prime Minister is usually the leader of the party who has won the most seats at a general election.

QUIZ TIME

Can you answer these questions about the story? There are answers at the end (but no peeking before you finish!)

1. Why did Sam think the headteacher would not be cross with him?

    A she was his auntie

    B she was his mum

    C he was always well behaved

2. What does Sam say is strange about the headteacher's reflection?

    A she has two

    B it is not her

    C she doesn't have one

3. Why does Monkey get a lunchtime detention?

    A he stuck his tongue out at a teacher

    B his uniform was a mess

    C he was late to school

4. What did Monkey use to see the evil white-boned demon?

   A demon-detecting glasses

   B fiery-eyes glasses

   C red-hot glasses

5. Why does Sandy think there is no point calling the police?

   A they would be too busy

   B they wouldn't get there in time

   C they wouldn't believe them

6. What shape does Monkey shift into first?

   A fly

   B bee

   C bird

7. How did they get into the storeroom?

   A Sandy whispered a magic spell

   B Zu picked the lock

   C Monkey whispered a magic spell

8. What did Monkey take from his body to make 3 of him?

   A 3 hairs

   B 8 hairs

   C 5 hairs

What Next?

If you enjoyed reading this story and haven't already read *Skate Monkey: Kidnap*, grab yourself a copy and curl up somewhere to read it!

1A, 2C, 3B, 4B, 5C, 6A, 7C, 8A

Answers to 'Quiz Time'